ELMER and GRANDPA ELDO

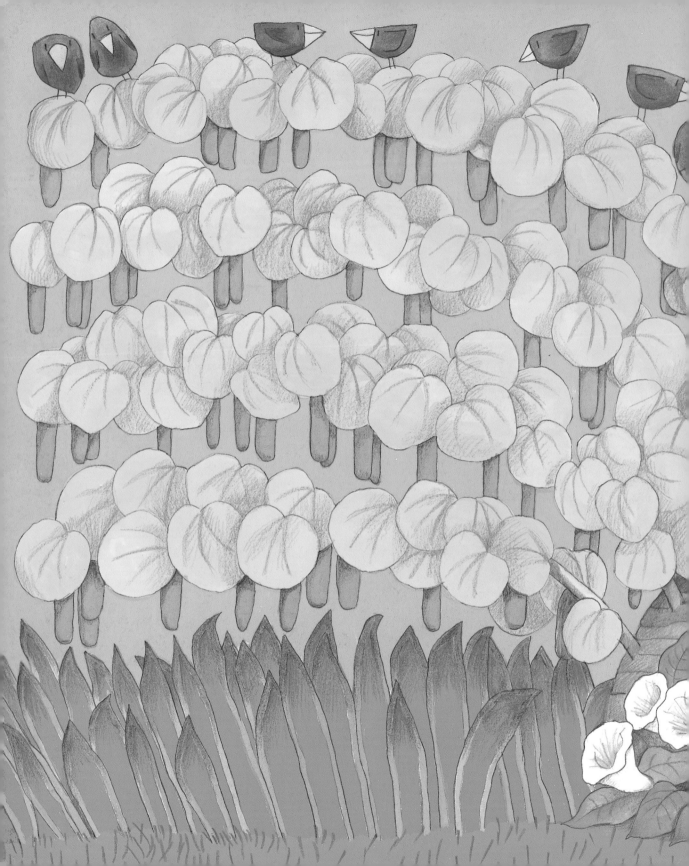

for Charlotte and Antoine

ELMER AND GRANDPA ELDO
A Red Fox Book: 978 0 099 43215 9

Published by Red Fox, an imprint of Random House Children's Books

First published in Great Britain by Andersen Press Ltd 2001
Red Fox edition published 2002

3 5 7 9 10 8 6 4

Red Fox Books are published by Random House Children's Books,
61-63 Uxbridge Road, London W5 5SA,
a division of The Random House Group, Ltd,
in Australia by Random House Australia (Pty) Ltd,
20 Alfred Street, Milsons Point, Sydney, NSW 2061, Australia,
in New Zealand by Random House New Zealand Ltd,
18 Poland Road, Glenfield, Auckland 10, New Zealand,
and in South Africa by Random House (Pty) Ltd,
Isle of Houghton, Corner Boundary Road & Carse O'Gowrie, Houghton 2198, South Africa

THE RANDOM HOUSE GROUP Limited Reg. No. 954009
www.rbooks.co.uk

A CIP catalogue record for this book is available from the British Library.

Printed in Singapore

ELMER and GRANDPA ELDO

David McKee

RED FOX

Elmer, the patchwork elephant, was picking fruit.

"Picking fruit, Elmer?" asked a monkey.

"I'm going to see Grandpa Eldo and this is his favourite," said Elmer.

"Golden Grandpa Eldo," said Monkey. "That's nice."

Grandpa Eldo was pleased to see Elmer.
"What a lovely surprise," he said. "What's that
balanced on your head?"

"Your favourite fruit," said Elmer,
"Fancy you remembering that," said Eldo.
"I remember lots of things," said Elmer.

"What else do you remember?" asked Eldo.

"The walks we used to go on," said Elmer.

"Walks? Where did we go?" Eldo asked.

"Don't you remember?" said Elmer. "I'll show you. Come on."

"We used to come this way, past the rocks," said Elmer.
"Here I used to hide, then jump out and shout . . ."
Elmer turned around, but Eldo wasn't there. "Grandpa?
Grandpa Eldo, where are you?" he called.

Eldo suddenly jumped out in front of Elmer.
"BOOH!" he shouted.

"Oh, Grandpa!" Elmer laughed. "I was supposed to do that.
Come on, now we go down to the stream."

At the stream Elmer said, "Don't you remember anything? We used to play stepping stones."
"Show me," said Eldo.

There were already some rocks in the water.
Elmer added more to fill in the spaces. "Now walk across,"
he said. "Be careful, there's usually a wobbly one."

Suddenly there was a huge SPLASH! Elmer had fallen in.
"You were right. You've a good memory," Eldo chuckled.
Elmer laughed. "Lucky it's not deep."
"Now where?" asked Eldo.
"You still don't remember," said Elmer. "To the lake, of course."

"We used to play Ducks and Drakes," said Elmer. He picked up a flat stone and sent it skipping across the water. "Seven splashes," he said.

"Let me try," said Eldo.

"You need a nice flat stone," said Elmer, but Eldo had already thrown. "1,2,3,4,5,6,7,8,9," they counted together.

When they set off again, Elmer started to sing.
Eldo joined in, then the birds joined in too.

"When we're marching on our way,
bumpity bump, bumpity bump.
We like to laugh and play,
bumpity bump, bumpity bump.
And when we can't think what to do
We simply hide and then shout, 'BOOOOH!'
When we're marching on our way,
bumpity bump, bumpity bump!"

When they shouted, "BOOH!" the birds flew
around squawking with laughter.

It started to rain and they dashed into a cave for shelter. "Surely you remember the stories you used to tell me?" Elmer asked.

Eldo frowned. "What were they?" he asked.

"*Red Riding Hood, Jack and the Beanstalk, Cinderella, Three Little Pigs* . . . Mmmm . . . *Billygoats Gruff* . . . Aaaah . . . *Sleeping Beauty* . . ." Elmer hesitated.

"*Hansel and Gretel, Tom Thumb, Goldilocks* . . ." Eldo continued.

"You cheat, you do remember!" said Elmer.

Eldo laughed and, now the rain had stopped,
ran off. Elmer chased him all the way back to Eldo's
place shouting, "You tricked me. You remembered
everything. I'll get you, Grandpa Eldo."

After they had their breath back, and stopped laughing, and finished the fruit that Elmer brought, it was time to go home.

"It's been fun, Grandpa," said Elmer. "You really remembered everything, didn't you?"

"Yes," chuckled Eldo. "And I was so happy that you did, too. But best of all, you remembered to visit me."

Elmer smiled, "'Bye, Grandpa," he said. "See you soon."

Other **ELMER** books to enjoy:

ELMER 0099697203

ELMER AGAIN 0099917203

ELMER ON STILTS 0099296713

ELMER IN THE SNOW 0099721317

ELMER AND THE WIND 0099402637

ELMER'S HIDE-AND-SEEK 0099410982

ELMER AND THE LOST TEDDY 0099404168

ELMER'S CONCERT 0099503212

LOOK! THERE'S ELMER 0099432064

Bath Books:

ELMER'S BATH 0099503417

ELMER'S SPLASH 0099503514

Mini hardbacks:

ELMER IN THE SNOW 0862649129

ELMER AND WILBUR 0862649110

Other books by David McKee in Red Fox

CHARLOTTE'S PIGGY BANK

ISABEL'S NOISY TUMMY

MARY'S SECRET

NOT NOW, BERNARD

TUSK TUSK

TWO MONSTERS

PRINCE PETER AND THE TEDDY BEAR